Charles Villiers Stanford, Robert Louis Stevenson

A Child's Garland of Songs

gathered from A child's garden of verses

Charles Villiers Stanford, Robert Louis Stevenson

A Child's Garland of Songs
gathered from A child's garden of verses

ISBN/EAN: 9783337100575

Printed in Europe, USA, Canada, Australia, Japan

Cover: Foto ©Andreas Hilbeck / pixelio.de

More available books at **www.hansebooks.com**

A CHILD'S GARLAND
OF SONGS

GATHERED FROM

A CHILD'S GARDEN OF VERSES

BY

ROBERT LOUIS STEVENSON

AND SET TO MUSIC

BY

C. VILLIERS STANFORD.
Op. 30

London :
Longmans, Green, & Co.,
And New York : 15 East 16th Street.
1892

To

GERALDINE and GUY.

INTRODUCTION.

COME, my little children, here are songs for you,
  Some are short, and some are long, and all, all are new.
You must learn to sing them very small and clear,
Very true to time and tune, and pleasing to the ear.

Mark the note that rises, mark the notes that fall,
Mark the time when broken, and the swing of it all.
So when night is come, and you have gone to bed,
All the songs you love to sing shall echo in your head.

R. L. S.

INDEX.

✳ ✳ ✳

BED IN SUMMER

Allegretto semplice.

dress by yel _ low can _ dle - light............ In sum _ mer, quite the

o _ ther way, I have to go to bed by day.

I have to go to bed and see The birds still hop _ ping on the tree,

Or hear the grown - up peo _ ple's feet Still

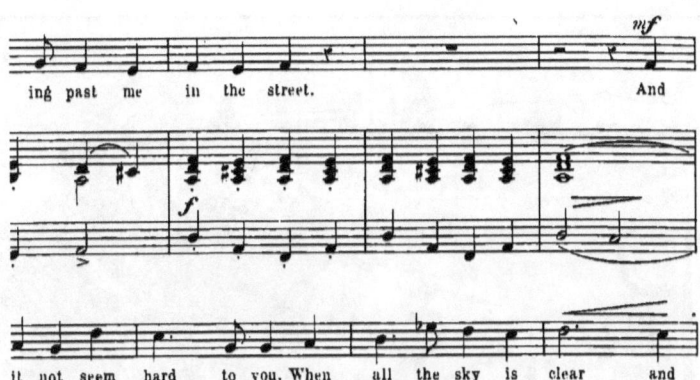

ing past me in the street. And

it not seem hard to you, When all the sky is clear and

5

Winds are in the air, they are blow_ing in the spring,......... And

waves are on the mea_dow like the waves there are at sea.

Where shall we ad_ven _ ture, to-day that we're a_

float,......... Wa _ ry of the wea _ ther and steer _ ing by a

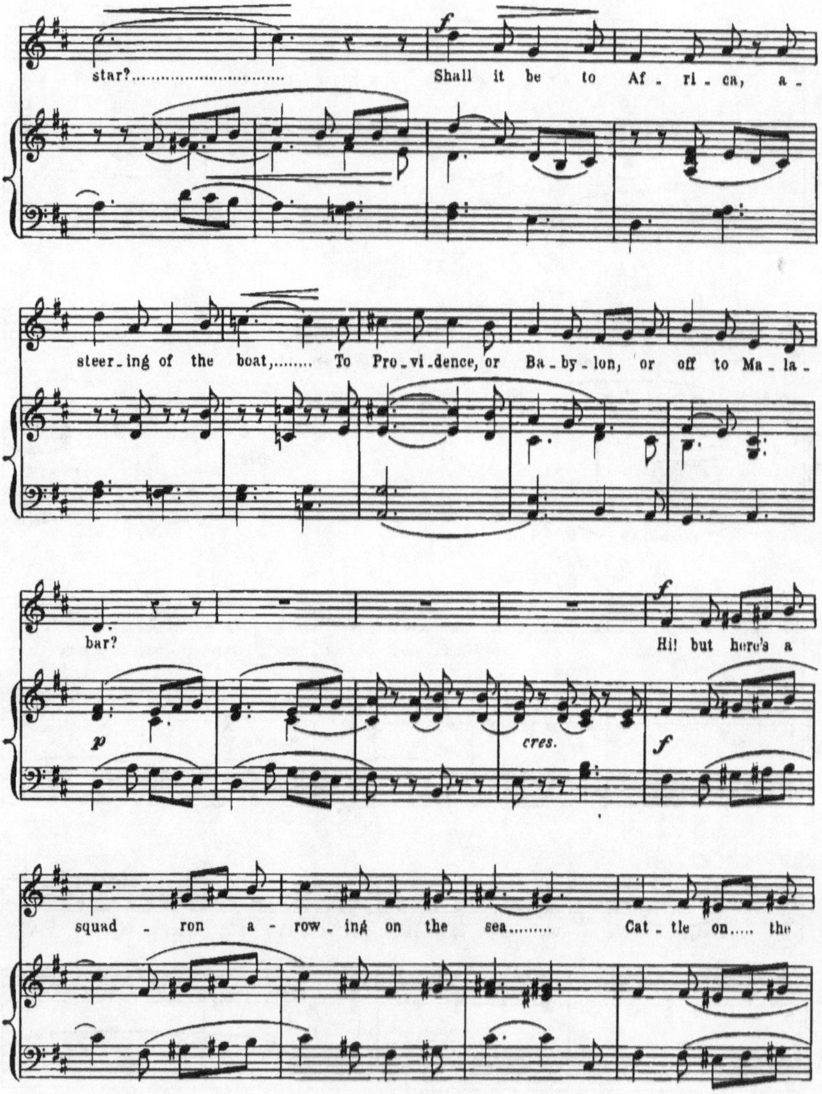
f
star?.............................. Shall it be to Af - ri - ca, a -
steer - ing of the boat,........ To Pro - vi - dence, or Ba - by - lon, or off to Ma - la -
bar?
f
Hi! but here's a
p
cres.
f
squad - ron a - row - ing on the sea......... Cat - tle on..... the

mea _ dow a – charging with a roar! Quick, and we'll es _

cape them, they're as mad as they can be,........ The

wick _ et is the har _ bour and the gar _ den is the

shore.

FOREIGN LANDS.

Andante.

p

Up in - to the cher - ry tree

Who should climb but lit - tle me? I held the trunk with

both my hands And look'd a_broad on for _ eign lands.

I saw the next door gar _ den lie, A _ dorn'd with flow'rs, be_

fore my eye, And

10

many plea - sant pla - ces more That I had nev - er

seen be - fore.

I saw the dimp - ling

riv - er pass And be the sky's blue look - ing - glass; The

dus _ ty roads go up and down With peo _ ple tramp _ ing

in _ to town.

If I could find a

high _ er tree...... Far _ ther and far _ ther I should

12

land,

Where all the child _ ren dine at five, And

all the play _ things come..... a _ live,...............

WINDY NIGHTS

Allegro molto.

When - ev - er the moon and the stars are set, When - ev - er the wind is high, All night long in the dark and wet, A man goes rid - ing by.

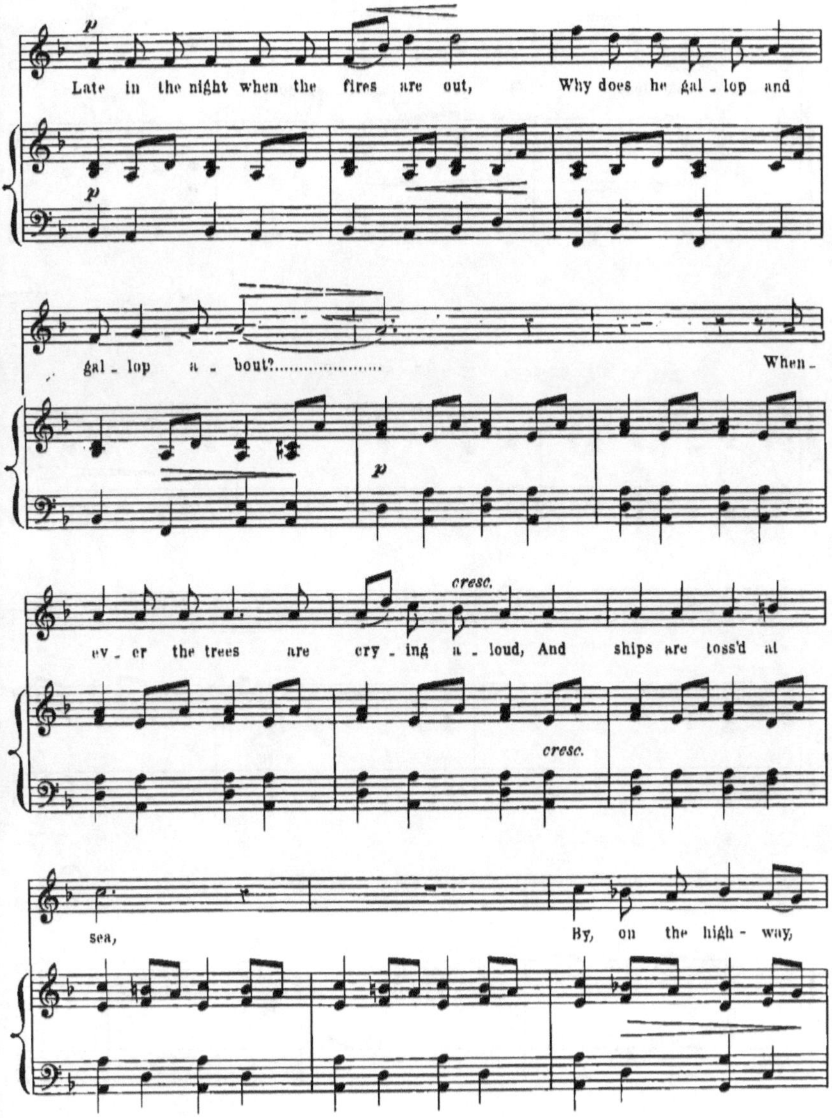
p
Late in the night when the fires are out,
Why does he gal - lop and
p
gal - lop a - bout?......................
When -
p
cresc.
ev - er the trees are cry - ing a - loud, And ships are toss'd at
cresc.
sea,
By, on the high - way,

low and loud, By at the gal _ lop goes he.

_, at the gal _ lop he goes, and then

By he comes back at the gal _ lop a _ gain.....................

dim.

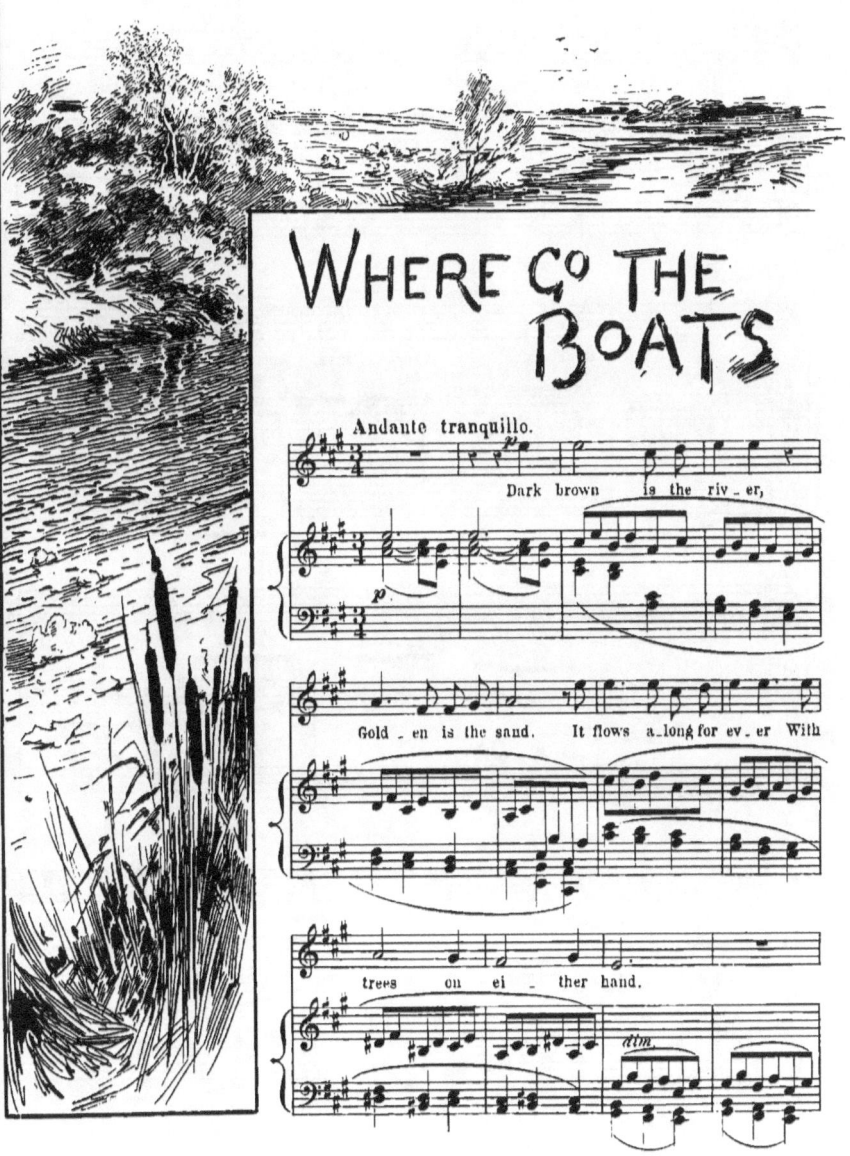

WHERE GO THE BOATS

Green leaves a - float _ ing, Cas _ tles of the foam,......................

Boats of mine a - boat _ ing __ Where.................. will all come

home? On goes the

riv _ er And out past the mill, A _ way down the val _ ley, A_

way............ down the hill. A_

way down the riv_er, A hun_dred miles or more,................

O _ ther lit_tle chil_dren Shall bring................. my boats a_shore.

very, very like me from the heels up to the head;
some-times shoots up tall-er like an in-dia-rub-ber ball,
stays so close be-side me, he's a cow-ard you can see;

And I see him jump be-fore me, when I
And he some-times gets so lit-tle that there's
I'd think shame to stick to nur-sie as that

jump in-to my bed.
none of him at all.
sha-dow sticks to me!

poco più lento p

4. One

morn_ing, ve_ry ear_ly, be_fore the sun was up, I rose and found the shin_ing dew...

sempre più lento

on ev'_ry but_ter_cup; But my la_zy lit_tle sha_dow, like an

ar_rant sleep_y-head, Had stayed at home be_hind me and was

fast....... a_sleep in bed.

MARCHING SONG.

Allegro alla Marcia.

Bring the comb and play upon it! Marching here we come!

Will_lie cocks his highland bon_net,

John _ nie beats the drum.

Ma _ ry Jane com _ mands the par _ ty, Pet _ er leads the rear;

Feet in time, a _ lert and hear _ ty, Each a Gren _ a _ dier!

All in the most mar_tial man_ner

March_ing dou_ble-quick;

While the nap_kin like a ban_ner   Waves.................... up_on the

Great com - man - der Jane!   Now that we've been round   the vil - lage,

Let's   go   home.......... a - gain.

dim.

dim. sempre

FOREIGN CHILDREN.

Lento espressivo.

Lit_tle In_dian, Sioux or Crow, Lit_tle frost_y Es_ki_mo, Lit_tle

Turk or Ja_pan_ee, O! don't you wish that you were me? You have

seen the scar_let trees And the li_ons o_ver seas; You have eat_en ostrich

eggs, And turn'd the tur_tles off their legs. Such a

life...... is ve_ry fine, But it's not so nice as mine: You must

of_ten, as you trod, Have wear_ied not to be a_broad.

You have cu_riousthings to eat, I am fed on pro_per

meat; You must dwell be-yond the foam, But I am safe and live at home.

Lento espressivo.

Lit_tle In_dian, Sioux or Crow;

Lit_tle fros_ty Es_ki_mo,

Lit_tle Turk or Ja_pa_nee, O! don't you wish that you were me?

MY SHIP AND ME.

Allegro giojoso.

mf

1. O it's I that am the cap _ tain of a ti _ dy lit _ tle ship, Of a
2. For I mean to grow as lit _ tle as the dol _ ly at the helm, And the

ship that goes a - sail _ ing on the pond; And my
dol _ ly I in _ tend to come a _ live; And with

ship it keeps a-turn-ing all a-round and all a-bout; But when
him be-side to help me, it's a-sail-ing I shall go, It's a-

I'm a lit-tle old-er, I shall find the se-cret out............
sail-ing on the wa-ter, when the jol-ly breez-es blow............

How to send my ves-sel sail-ing on be-yond.
And the ves-sel goes a-di-vie-di-vie-dive.

3. O it's

then you'll see me sail_ing thro' the rush_es and the reeds, And you'll

hear the wa_ter sing_ing at the prow; For be_

cres.

side the dol_ly sai_lor, I'm to voy_age and ex_plore, To

rall. un poco   *a tempo*

land up_on the is_land where no dol_ly was be_fore,.....................

colla voce   *a tempo*

And to fire the pen _ ny can _ non in the bow.

sf

p · rall. molto

sf

www.ingramcontent.com/pod-product-compliance
Lightning Source LLC
Chambersburg PA
CBHW030912260626
47169CB00008B/2816